Given In Honor Of

Mrs. Jacobi
Student Council

By

Mrs. Cox

School   Stony Creek Elementary

Date   1999-2000

HURRICANE!

JONATHAN LONDON ✦ HENRI SORENSEN

Lothrop, Lee & Shepard Books ✦ Morrow
New York

Oil paints were used for the full-color illustrations. The text type is 16-point Bitstream Cooper Light.

Text copyright © 1998 by Jonathan London
Illustrations copyright © 1998 by Henri Sorensen

Based on "Noche de Paz," a short story first published in the April 1995 edition of *Cricket* magazine.

Published by Lothrop, Lee & Shepard Books
an imprint of Morrow Junior Books, a division of William Morrow and Company, Inc., 1350 Avenue of the Americas, New York, NY 10019
www.williammorrow.com

Printed in the United States of America.

10 9 8 7 6 5 4 3 2 1

Library of Congress Cataloging-in-Publication Data
London, Jonathan.
Hurricane!/by Jonathan London; illustrated by Henri Sorensen.
p. cm.
Summary: A young boy describes the experiences of his family when a hurricane hits their home on the island of Puerto Rico.
ISBN 0-688-12977-3 (trade)—ISBN 0-688-12978-1 (library)
[1. Hurricanes—Fiction. 2. Puerto Rico—Fiction.] I. Sorensen, Henri, ill. II. Title. PZ7.L84321Is 1998 [E]—DC20 94-14518 CIP AC

For my brother, Jeff,
who was there with me
—JL

For Jonathan, Alberto,
Philip, and Birgitte Serejo
—HS

The day of the hurricane started a lot like any other day. After breakfast, Jeff and I checked our shoes for scorpions, then went outside to play.

El Yunque, the biggest mountain in Puerto Rico, loomed over us as we scrambled down the cliff to the ocean. The breeze was soft and the sea was calm inside the coral reef. Far out, a giant stingray flapped its wings across the waves. Our fins slapped as we waded in, watching for the sharp black spines of sea urchins.

We pulled our masks down, kicked out toward the reef breathing through our snorkels, and dived down. Sea fans waved. Fire corals flamed. Schools of tropical fish flashed by like flocks of birds turning in a wind, while *langostas*—tasty Puerto Rican lobsters—hid in dark cracks in the huge reef.

We came up for breath—and everything around
us had changed. The sky had turned deep purple,
crowded with clouds. The air was perfectly still, with
not a whisper of breeze. I felt as if my breath were
being sucked from my lungs.

We swam ashore and climbed up the rocks. Mom raced from the house. "A hurricane!" she panted. "It's coming our way!" Our house could be blown right off its stilts. "Hurry up," Mom told us. "Pack quickly!"

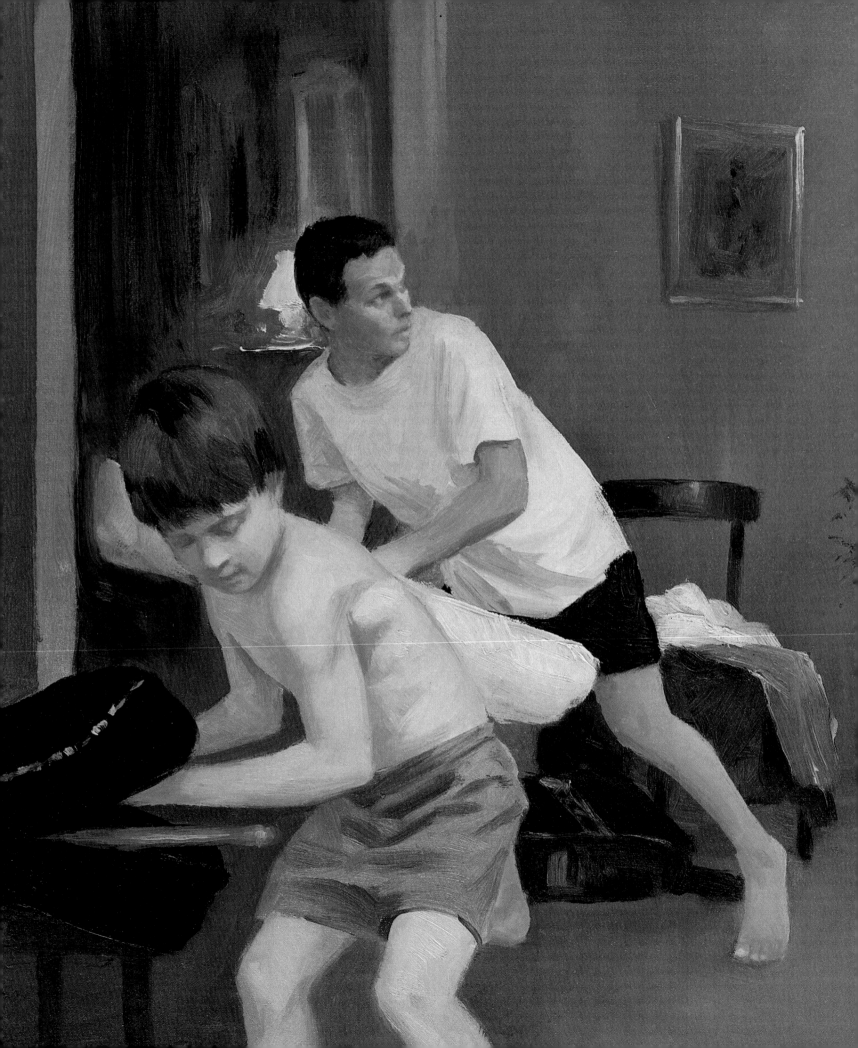

I ran inside and packed my baseball mitt and ball,
my shooting marbles, Slinky, and yo-yo.

Then I rushed out to put my bike away.

Fists of wind pounded me, punching me sideways.
The palm trees bent and thrashed in a wild dance. The
wind was pushing the waves into mountains. They
broke over the coral reef, then crashed against the
rocks in a burst of spray as high as our cliff.

"Batten down the hatches!" Dad shouted in his old
navy talk as he slammed the storm shutters.

I tried to whistle for Triste, but no sound came.

The sky was alive. Lightning scribbled on the dark clouds that had buried El Yunque. Thunder shook the earth.

Suddenly, Triste leaped into my arms and almost knocked me down. The palms, whipping crazily, slung coconuts at us.

Everyone piled into the car. I was crammed into the backseat beside Jeff and a suitcase. Triste sat on my lap and whimpered.

The moment Dad drove off, the sky fell. Rain
slammed into us like a crashing wave. All the way to
the shelter, we drove through rain so solid, it was like
driving underwater.

The shelter was an old navy barracks where
sailors used to live. Babies cried and grown-ups
bustled around and kids yelled at one another. I sat
on a sagging bunk bed and hugged Triste.

Suddenly, with a loud crash, the wind ripped a
shutter off. Glass shattered. The hurricane roared in as
the lights went out.

Mom lit a kerosene lamp. Dad and two other men shoved some metal lockers in front of the broken window. I helped, too. The barracks shivered and creaked like an old ship at sea. Nails squeaked in the wood as if they were trying to hold the whole building together.

Somebody started to sing, so quietly at first that I thought I was just hearing things. But her voice grew stronger. Jeff joined in, then my folks and I. Soon everybody in the shelter was singing "Silent Night." *"Noche de paz…noche de amor…"* Christmas was months away, but no one cared. The singing made us feel better.

Finally, halfway through the night, the wind died
down. The rain stopped hammering. All was silent.
"Well, it's over," Dad said. Mom gave me a big hug.

When we got home, the yard was littered with coconuts and palm fronds. But the roof was still on our house, and our house was still on its stilts. We were lucky. We heard on the radio that just fifty miles away, a tin shack shantytown had been flattened by wind and waves.

The next morning, Jeff and I started cleaning up our
yard. The sky and sea were rosy and calm. Above us,
unbelievably green, stood El Yunque. It was tall and
peaceful as ever, as if nothing at all had happened.
"*¡Vámonos!*" I shouted to Jeff. "Let's go!"